THE Merry Christmas BOOK

(Christmas Songs and Stories)

Stories by
JEAN HORTON BERG

Pictures by
CATHERINE SCHOLZ

Music Arranged by
DOROTHY B. COMMINS

WONDER BOOKS • NEW YORK

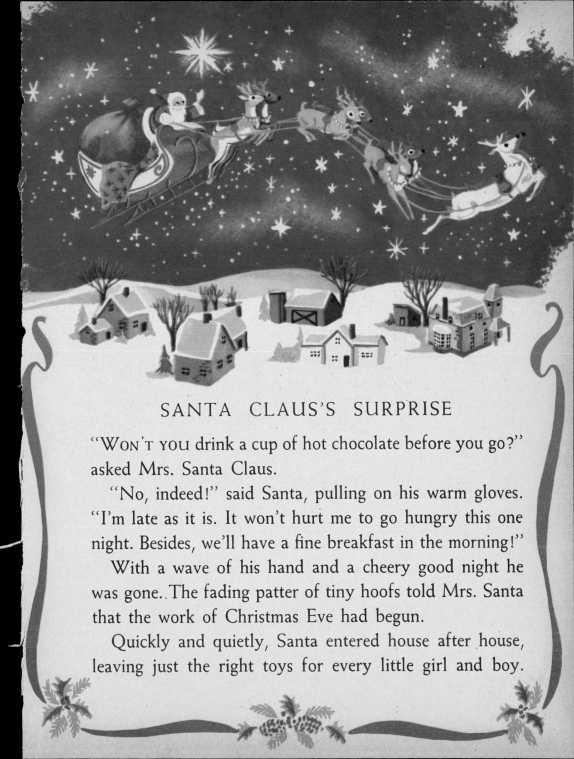

SANTA CLAUS'S SURPRISE

"WON'T YOU drink a cup of hot chocolate before you go?" asked Mrs. Santa Claus.

"No, indeed!" said Santa, pulling on his warm gloves. "I'm late as it is. It won't hurt me to go hungry this one night. Besides, we'll have a fine breakfast in the morning!"

With a wave of his hand and a cheery good night he was gone. The fading patter of tiny hoofs told Mrs. Santa that the work of Christmas Eve had begun.

Quickly and quietly, Santa entered house after house, leaving just the right toys for every little girl and boy.

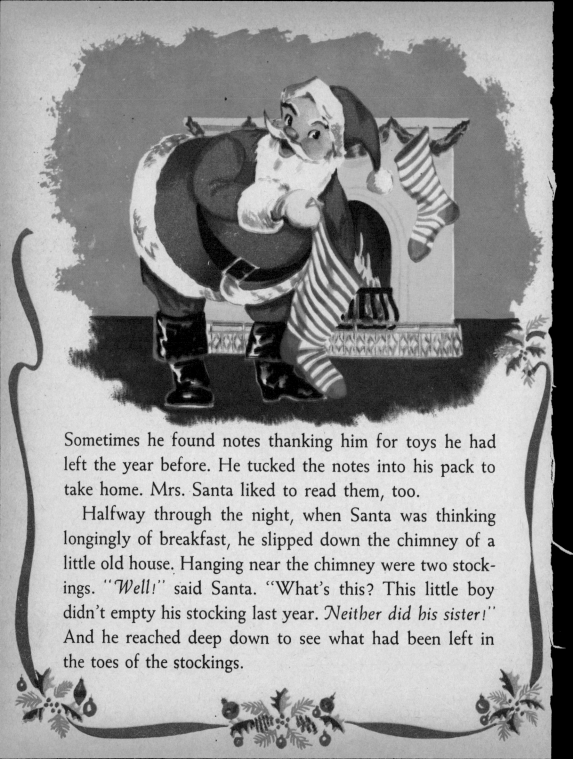

Sometimes he found notes thanking him for toys he had left the year before. He tucked the notes into his pack to take home. Mrs. Santa liked to read them, too.

Halfway through the night, when Santa was thinking longingly of breakfast, he slipped down the chimney of a little old house. Hanging near the chimney were two stockings. *"Well!"* said Santa. "What's this? This little boy didn't empty his stocking last year. *Neither did his sister!"* And he reached deep down to see what had been left in the toes of the stockings.

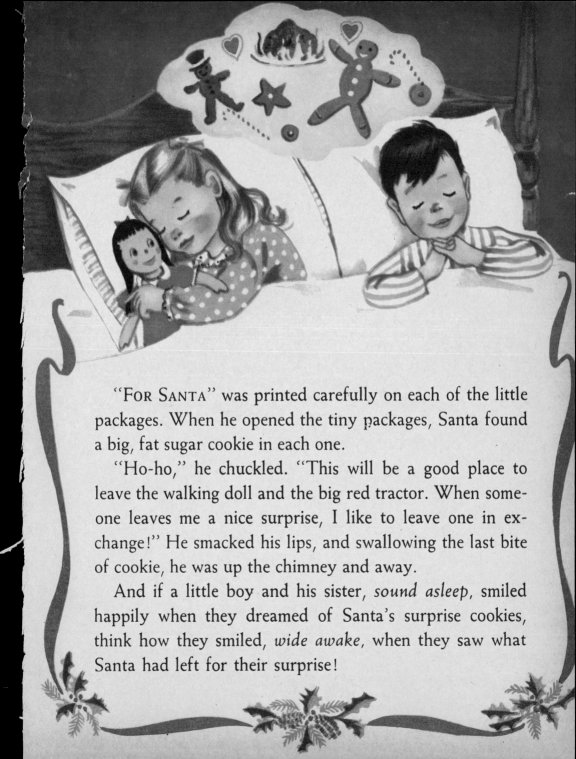

"FOR SANTA" was printed carefully on each of the little packages. When he opened the tiny packages, Santa found a big, fat sugar cookie in each one.

"Ho-ho," he chuckled. "This will be a good place to leave the walking doll and the big red tractor. When someone leaves me a nice surprise, I like to leave one in exchange!" He smacked his lips, and swallowing the last bite of cookie, he was up the chimney and away.

And if a little boy and his sister, *sound asleep*, smiled happily when they dreamed of Santa's surprise cookies, think how they smiled, *wide awake*, when they saw what Santa had left for their surprise!

SILENT NIGHT

Words by Joseph Mohr

Si - lent night! Ho - ly night! All is calm, all is bright

Round yon Vir - gin Moth-er and Child, Ho - ly In-fant so ten-der and mild;

Sleep in heav-en-ly peace. Sleep in heav - en - ly peace.

TOY SHOP

THE BRIDE DOLL AND THE DRUM

"I HOPE no one buys me," the Bride Doll whispered to the little Red Drum in the toy shop. "Think what I'd look like if a little girl with sticky fingers were to get me! I ought to stand safely on a shelf!"

"I'd like to be beaten," said the Drum. "I'm afraid I'll forget how to rattity-tum!"

Just then a nice-looking young man walked into the shop and looked around. Suddenly he spied the Doll.

"Ha!" he cried. "Just what I've been looking for! Patsy will love her. And what's this? *A drum!* A RED DRUM! I'll take them both."

And before they knew it, the Bride Doll and the Drum were bundled into boxes and whisked away.

On Christmas morning eager little fingers opened the boxes. "Oooooooooo!" squealed Patsy. "Uncle John has given me a Bride Doll! She's so beautiful she must stand in the very center of my shelf!"

Brother Bobby didn't hear her. He was too busy practicing rattity-tums on his new Red Drum.

But in spite of the noise he was making, the little Red Drum heard the Bride Doll whisper, "Isn't this a happy day? We all have what we wanted!"

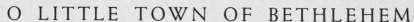

O LITTLE TOWN OF BETHLEHEM

Words by Phillips Brooks

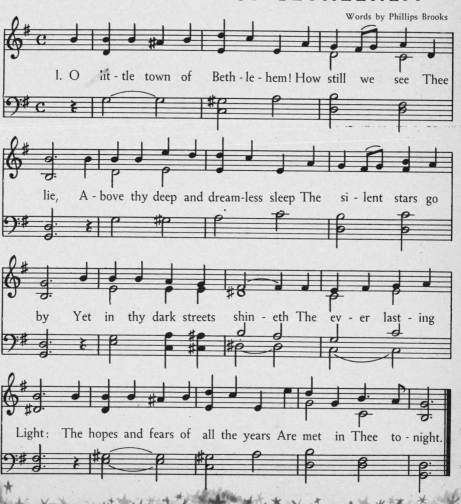

1. O lit-tle town of Beth-le-hem! How still we see Thee lie, A-bove thy deep and dream-less sleep The si-lent stars go by Yet in thy dark streets shin-eth The ev-er last-ing Light: The hopes and fears of all the years Are met in Thee to-night.

SPOT'S CHRISTMAS PRESENT

THE MOMENT Jody spied Spot peeking out of Daddy's pocket, he knew the little puppy was something special. And he was right! You can't imagine how quickly Spot learned to chase a baseball, and to bring the evening paper up the front steps, and to sit up and beg when he wanted a puppy biscuit.

But Spot couldn't speak. He couldn't bark at all!

If another dog came into the yard, Spot pranced and played—without a bark! When the grocery boy came, Spot ran round in circles until he was dizzy—without a bark!

Christmas Eve, when Jody hung up his stocking, he hung up a stocking for Spot, too.

"I suppose he'll get a toy," Jody said to his mother. "But what Spot really needs is a good loud bark!"

Christmas morning when Jody took down the stockings, there *was* a toy in Spot's stocking. It was a little rubber dog.

Spot circled it once or twice. Then he pounced on it.

"Waaaaaaaaaaaah!" The little rubber dog squeaked so loudly that Spot's ears flew straight up.

Spot pounced on the toy again. Once more the little rubber dog squeaked. But this time there was another sound.

"Woooooooof!" *Spot had woofed!* He rolled right over in surprise. Then he raced round and round the room. "Woof-woof-woof!" Spot barked. And that night, when he snuggled into the cozy box at the foot of Jody's bed, he tried one last little *woof*—just to make sure he hadn't forgotten how to do it.

"This is a Christmas we'll remember," said Jody. "This is the Christmas Spot got his bark!"

JINGLE BELLS

Words by J. Pierpont

THE HAPPY LITTLE FIR TREE

EVER SINCE the little Fir Tree had grown tall enough to peek into the Bakers' living-room window, she had loved Christmas. She liked watching Mrs. Baker dress the fireplace with greens. She liked seeing the Christmas tree glittering with bright glass balls and tinsel. And she loved watching the children unwrap their presents. The only thing the little Fir Tree did not like was being outdoors and not sharing in all the fun.

But *this* Christmas, before breakfast, Mr. Baker and Sue and Harry went outdoors and trimmed the little Fir

Tree. They fastened a round dish of food that birds like
to a sturdy branch. They tied strips of suet and doughnuts
to the upper branches, and juicy carrots to the lower
branches. In no time at all the birds and squirrels and
bunnies gathered for a treat.

Now the little Fir Tree was truly happy. For, while she
watched the fun going on indoors, she was sharing Christmas with her friends, feathered and furry, outdoors!

DECK THE HALL

Old Welsh Air

Deck the hall with boughs of hol - ly, Fa la la la la, la la, la la.

Tis the sea - son to be jol - ly, Fa la la la la, la la, la, la.

Don we now our gay ap-par - el, Fa la la la la, la la, la, la.

Troll the an-cient Yule-tide car-ol, Fa la la la la, la la, la, la.

THE SURPRISE IN JOHNNY'S STOCKING

"Nobody ever had such a wonderful Christmas," said Johnny, looking at the presents piled beneath the Christmas tree—the toolbox from Grandma and Grandpa, the pencils from Santa with J-O-H-N-N-Y spelled out in gold letters, and the cowboy suit from Mother and Daddy.

"Aren't you going to look in your stocking?" Mother asked.

In a moment Johnny was sitting on the floor pulling presents from the stocking. He took out a blue top, a pack of trading cards, and a wooden whistle. And down at the very toe of the stocking he found a piece of paper.

"What's this?" asked Johnny.

"Read it," said Daddy.

"LOOK IN THE PANTRY," Johnny read.

The paper fluttered to the floor as Johnny raced to the pantry. In a moment he returned, pulling a shiny red wagon. "Won't everyone be surprised when I tell them that I found a red wagon in my stocking!" Johnny cried.

AWAY IN A MANGER

Words by Martin Luther

A - way in a man - ger, no crib for a bed, The lit - tle Lord

Je - sus laid down His sweet head, The stars in the sky looked

down where He lay, The lit - tle Lord Je-sus a - sleep on the hay.